THE 11TH FLOOR

CHARLES CULVER

Copyright Information

ISBN: 978-1-105-69963-4

Need to contact the author? You may contact the author by one of the following ways.

Email: info@chuckculver.com
Website: http://www.chuckculver.com

Introduction

For many years now, I have had some fairly disturbing nightmares. This book will probably be the first of many where I turn those nightmares into stories. I hope everyone reading this will enjoy the work that my subconscious mind cranks out while I am asleep.

I also would like to thank everyone who supported and encouraged me during the writing of my first book. First, my mother, Susan, deserves a lot of credit. Every time I completed a few chapters, I would send them to her for a review and opinion. Second, my wife Tamsen, who never even read one sentence of this until I was done. She read the whole thing and pointed out every mistake I made. So if there are more, you can blame her. Kidding.

I would also like to give some kudos to James Baldini. He is a good friend of mine who also recently just wrote and published his first book. Whether he knows it or not, he was my inspiration for actually getting this book done. His success provided some of my motivation. When you are done reading this story, check out his book. "The Book of Virtues, Volume 1."

Enjoy.

Chapter 1

He woke up screaming. His forehead was drenched in sweat. Wiping his head with his sleeve, he quickly looked around the room.

"Great. Where am I now?" he asked.

Fumbling through his pockets he retrieved his cell phone and opened the flashlight app. The bright LED light lit the room and from what he could tell, he was alone, except for the headless body on the floor next to him. He screamed again.

Beginning around the age of nineteen, Luke had been experiencing occasional nighttime blackouts. A few years later, on the advice of his girlfriend at the time, he saw several doctors and had numerous tests performed. Not a single medical expert was able to find a cause for his condition. The best treatment anyone could suggest was to refrain from eating a few hours before bed, do not imbibe alcohol or drugs, and avoid stressful daily activities. More than one doctor suggested exercise and a little bit of weight loss might be wise. Their suggestions did help ease the occurrences, but did not cure his ailment.

Over the years, he kept himself in terrific health and was pretty much the ideal weight for his height - one hundred eighty five pounds and six foot tall. He ran a few miles a couple times a week, and lifted weights occasionally. He never drank or used drugs. In fact, he was rarely ever sick, but none of that seemed to matter.

He was now thirty-three years old and the night blackouts continued. He could only ever remember going to sleep and the subsequent nightmares that followed. The nightmares typically featured demons, spirits, ghosts, murderers and other subjects of the macabre. When he would awaken, he would always find himself somewhere other than his own bed. Since he lived by himself in a studio apartment, he had no one to ask about what may have happened. He once tried to videotape himself while sleeping, but it proved to be a waste of effort. Upon review of the tape, it only showed him getting out of bed and turning the camera off, which he did not remember doing.

On a list of places he had found himself upon waking, next to a dead body was the most terrifying. In the past he had awakened under a tree in the woods, in a closet, back seat of a car, or even once on the bathroom floor of a highway rest stop. The bathroom floor was easily the most repulsive place Luke had ever found himself. This time was different. Not once in fourteen years had he ever woken up next to another person, living or dead.

He stared at the body with his cell phone light and became overwhelmed with fear. His hands shook. He switched off the light so he didn't have to see the dead person anymore. Having realized that with no light, he could not see the way out of the room, he quickly switched it back on and searched for a door. He found only a window with blackened panels.

The room itself was small with old brick walls. Some graffiti could be seen, but was too faded to read. It looked like there once was an unsuccessful attempt to remove or wash it off. There was a twin mattress on the floor in the corner, a small round coffee table, and a metal folding chair covered in blood. On the table were bits of hair, a few droplets of blood, and a blood covered bread knife. On the wall next to the table, carved into the brick, was written "Lord, save me. They are coming for me. I don't want to die." It looked fresh and recent. The brick shavings and dust were still present.

He headed back towards the window. He needed to get out of this room, now. The window was apparently the only exit.

Chapter 2

Tina lived at home with her parents. Upon graduating college, she was unable to find a job. Numerous applications and interviews yielded no work. Those were tough times indeed. With so many people out of work, every time a position opened up, the company was flooded with applicants. Plus, in attempts to save the company money, more and more programmer's jobs were offshored. Luckily, she had an "in" for a new opening. A large tech company was based in the nearby city, and her uncle Richie knew the owner.

When Tina woke that morning, she was both excited and nervous. She longed to move into an apartment of her own. She had been rehearsing answers to possible interview questions. When anyone had been through as many interviews as she, they notice common topics and questions. She didn't want to stutter or hesitate on an answer. Maybe they wouldn't place as much emphasis on the interview since her uncle knows the owner, she thought.

"Keep it together, Tina. You don't want to seem like a complete idiot in front of your new boss," she said to herself. "Well, potential new boss." She chuckled nervously.

She checked herself out in the mirror as she was putting on her makeup - stunning as usual, almost statuesque. She had long blonde hair, blue eyes, crazy curves, and beautiful long legs. She practically didn't even need to wear pantyhose.

As she was getting dressed, there was a knock on the wall of her room. Her mother usually knocked on the wall of the stairwell so she didn't have to go all the way up to the top to knock on her door. Her mother wasn't lazy; she just had knee and hip problems. The stairs were too much for her so she tried to stay downstairs as much as possible to avoid using them.

"Tina," her mother shouted. "Hurry up and come down for breakfast. You don't want to be late today."

"I'm coming! Be down shortly, Mommy," replied Tina.

Even though Tina was a grown woman of twenty-five, she still called her mother "Mommy". She felt childish sometimes, but it was a name that stuck. Not saying Mommy now felt wrong. Her mother didn't mind. In fact, she rather enjoyed it. Her father thought it was cute, as she called him "Daddy" too.

Her father called upstairs to her, "Yeah, hurry up kiddo. This train is leaving in fifteen minutes."

Her father was giving her a ride to the interview today since her car was in the shop. He drove an old Cadillac, which he jokingly referred to as the train, since it was so large and used massive amounts of fuel. Tina really wanted to buy a new car, but the banks didn't seem to give loans out to people with no income. This was at the top of her list of things to do once she got a job, along with the apartment. You can't move out on your own without a reliable means of transportation.

She quickly finished getting dressed and ran down the stairs for breakfast. She hoped it wasn't anything heavy, as she didn't have much of an appetite this morning. Luckily, her mother had prepared an assortment of fresh fruit and some dry wheat toast for her. Not many people would like that for breakfast, but she found it delightful.

Chapter 3

With his ear pressed up against the pane of glass, Luke heard nothing. He was unsure of where he was and his prior experiences told him not to barge into an unknown area without first checking for dangers. Besides, there was already a dead person in the room. Who knew what else might have been nearby. Not anxious to find out who or what killed the man, and not overly excited about possibly becoming dead himself if the suspect was still close, he listened a little longer.

Many years before during one of his blackouts, he had awakened in what appeared to be a walk-in pantry fully stocked with cans and boxes of food. Back then he wasn't as cautious as now, and carelessly threw open the door. Waiting on the other side was a dog, which had no doubt smelled him through the gap. He narrowly escaped being mauled that day by quickly jumping onto the countertop and going out the window.

Having listened for nearly ten minutes without hearing anything from the other side of the window, he cautiously pulled up on the handle and slid the window open about an inch. He peered through hoping not to see anyone or anything that might want to do him harm. There appeared to be no one around. In fact, it looked like the window backed up to a dead end alley in a city.

Fortunately for Luke, there was a fire escape alongside the window. He lifted himself up and sat on the windowsill, swung his legs around to the other side and dropped down onto the fire escape. He wanted to make as little noise as possible while he made his descent so as to not draw any unwanted attention. Silence proved a difficult task as this fire escape was old and rusty. He did make it safely to the ground, however noisy it may have been, and took off running down the alley as fast as he could.

While he was running, many questions came to mind. Why was there a room only accessible via a fire escape? What was this room used for? How did he end up there alone with a dead man? For that matter, who was that dead headless man and who killed him? Where was his head? Even with all these questions, he tried to focus on his primary goal at this point – get home and get there quickly.

As he approached the intersecting street, he slowed, caught his breath, and walked out of the alley. Once on the street, he glanced around looking for some kind of landmark or sign that might indicate where he was. Every direction he looked appeared the same. Nothing but tall buildings and empty cars were to be found. There were no people anywhere. In fact, there was no movement at all; no animals, birds, or sounds.

Luke said to himself, "Better get going in case someone or something heard that and comes looking for me."

Luke turned right and began walking down the empty street. That is when he noticed it out of the corner of his eye. There to his right, in a reflection of himself in the window of the storefront he was passing, was a hooded cloaked figure standing behind him. Startled, he staggered back, away from the window. Not immediately occurring to him was the fact that since it was a reflection, moving back away from it would mean that he was actually moving closer to the object behind him. Once he realized this, he spun around and found nothing was there.

Looking back over his shoulder yielded an entirely different image in the window than before. This was an image of a bustling street, filled with cars, and people all going about their daily lives, bathed in beautiful sunshine. It was like he was standing in the complete opposite of that picture. He closed his eyes tightly then opened them. One more look in the window revealed the street he was currently standing in, alone. This time there was no hooded figure behind him.

A chill came over Luke and goose bumps formed on his arms. Keeping quiet to listen for the approach of anyone or anything and not be caught by surprise, he walked cautiously down the street. Five minutes had passed before the noise began. Sounding like it was coming from every direction, completely surrounding him, there was maniacal laughter.

Chapter 4

Tina's father, Joseph, drove way too fast for her liking. She knew better than to say anything to him about it. Once before she commented on his driving and he responded with, "I've been driving longer than you have been alive." Besides, he had never gotten a ticket or been the cause of an accident, so she just sat quietly as a passenger and tried to enjoy the passing scenery.

Fortunately for her, it was a quick ride to the city. While they lived only twenty miles away in a nice rural community, the ride into the city typically took them almost ninety minutes. The roads they need to use to get to the highway were low speed limit roads. Once on the highway, they had to deal with congestion, bumper-to-bumper traffic, and lane closures on various bridges and tollbooths. The ride this day only took them thirty minutes. Traffic was nonexistent. Once in the city, Joseph parked the car in the first spot he found. While he was ecstatic that he managed to get a spot so easily, he was unnerved by what he saw.

Sitting in the now parked car, they both looked at each other, then at the empty streets almost in unison.

"Daddy," said Tina. "Where is everyone?"

"I don't know, kiddo, I have never seen anything like this before," said Joseph.

Tina just stared out the window. There was not a single person to be seen anywhere. She reached over and pushed down the button to control the window.

"I am not sure what to make of this," her father said. "There was no one on the way here, there's no one here now, and I'm betting that if we start driving around, we won't see anyone around the area at all."

"I don't like this, Daddy," Tina said as she finished putting the window down. "I don't hear any noise at all. It's like we drove into a ghost town."

"Ghost world is more like what I would describe it as," said Joseph. "Come to think of it, I haven't seen or heard from a single person since I woke up this morning, except for you and your mother."

"Oh my God, Mom," replied Tina as she reached into her purse to retrieve her cell phone. "I have to call her and make sure she is alright."

Tina dialed the numbers, pressed send, and was immediately greeted with a beeping noise. The screen read, "Call Failed. No Service." Cell service at her house was spotty and sometimes depended on the weather and season. If she had been at home, she may not have been surprised with the lack of signal; however, they were in the city. The city generally had nearly excellent signal strength and data speeds no matter where they were.

"Daddy, I have no signal on my phone. Try yours."

"I just did, mine is dead too."

He switched on the radio, but there was nothing but crackling noise and static across the entire band. Both AM and FM were dead.

"Do you think Mommy is okay?" she asked.

"I'm sure she is kiddo. Your mom is a trooper," replied Joseph. When we get home later, she'll probably be wondering why we didn't call with the good news of your interview."

"Do you think I should even still try going to my interview, I mean, considering there is no one around? I'm a little creeped out."

"No, don't you dare get out of this car," said Joseph. "I don't know what's going on. An entire city of people doesn't just disappear. I don't know what happened to them, and I don't want whatever it was to happen to us too."

No sooner had the words left his lips than they heard a demented laughter coming from outside the car.

Chapter 5

For the first time in five years, Jonathan woke up feeling completely rested. Living in the city was something you either loved or hated. He loved it, except for the constant noise. All day long he was surrounded by noise. All night long, there was more noise. Even in the middle of the night, you could hear it. Eventually it became part of your life and you began to tune it out and get used to it. Not Jonathan. He could deal with it during the day, but at night, he needed quiet.

Working as the CEO of a corporation with its headquarters in the city, he felt the need to live close by. He was a very hands-on kind of person and couldn't stand letting someone else make any decisions without his involvement. His position and wealth afforded him the ability to live in the city and not have to commute. His penchant for luxuries and his aversion to noise drove him to buy the top floor penthouse in a building near where he worked. Even as high as his apartment was located, he could still hear the city noise at night; however, the distance from the traffic and his white noise machine usually allowed him to sleep soundly at night.

He lived alone in his penthouse. He preferred solitude. It allowed him time to read books, think about life, and make business decisions. He did watch some television, but only business news channels. He never watched any of that reality show drivel that was so popular those days. His evening ritual was to read a few chapters of his current book of choice, then watch Bloomberg TV's recap on the day's events while enjoying a glass of scotch. His current favorite was The Macallan, 40-year. His father had taught him his appreciation of whiskey many years ago, before he passed away.

As Jonathan sat on the end of his bed pulling his socks on, he came to the sudden realization that it was quiet… much quieter than normal. In fact, he could not hear any of the cacophony normally produced by the city at this time of day. Mysteriously but pleasantly missing were the sounds of trucks and horns honking.

Stunned, he dropped his second sock, stood up, walked to the nearest window, and peered through the gap in the curtains. The window overlooked one of the city's busiest avenues. It appeared deserted. Quickly he ran back into his bedroom and into the closet. Digging through boxes, he retrieved a pair of binoculars that had been his fathers. While now considered antique, they provided a great magnification, unparalleled by most of the models that were on the market today.

Without hesitation, he rushed back to the same window, threw open the curtains, and peered down at the street. Same as without the binoculars, the street was empty. He could clearly see parked cars, but no drivers or pedestrians. Looking higher up into the windows of other buildings, he could not see anyone in offices or other apartments.

Then, a black object flashed past the front of the binoculars. It was too close to ascertain what exactly it was because he was focused on a distant building. It just appeared as a fast moving blur. Stepping back from the window a bit and lowering the binoculars, he saw it again, this time with clarity. Falling past his window were thousands of black birds, plummeting to the ground below.

Chapter 6

Living in a plastic covered refrigerator box, behind a dumpster at the end of an alley, isn't much of a home. Unfortunately for Eddie, it was all he had to call home. He'd had a long string of nothing but bad luck lately. A little more than a year before, he lost his job when the company went bankrupt. Shortly afterwards he got sick and the medical bills piled up. Unemployment eventually dried up and he found himself unable to pay the rent. He ended up getting evicted. He had already sold most everything he had to buy food, so he packed up what was left, some clothes and personal effects, and hit the streets. He didn't have any friends or family he could move in with. What little money he had, he spent on alcohol to help drown his sorrows. So he spent his free time, which was all his time, wandering around gathering cans and bottles, which he called his "salvageables" and stockpiling them next to his cardboard home.

That morning, Eddie was startled awake, not by the sound of a honking horn, or a garbage truck emptying his dumpster, but by the sound of metal creaking. The metal creaking was followed by a bang noise, a grunt, and footsteps running away. When he peeked around from outside his box, he saw a young man wearing jeans and a t-shirt running down the alley. He was really running fast, and he kept looking around as if he was expecting someone to be chasing him. When he reached the end of the alley, he stopped for a moment, turned right out onto the street, and walked away.

Eddie looked up at the fire escape and figured that is where the guy probably came from and what had made the metal noise. Following the escape ladder up, he noticed there was only one window at the top of it, and it was blacked out, but left open. The guy must have left via the window, but why was it black? Curiosity got the better of him so he decided to climb up and find out what was going on.

Luckily the ladder was already down so getting up there wasn't difficult. Upon climbing up the ladder and reaching the black window, he looked inside. Why would the man take off running down an alley after leaving an empty room? Nothing inside the room seemed worthy of running away from. Eddie saw nothing in there except a little girl's dolly. It was certainly ugly, but not scary, and it didn't make him want to run away. So why did the guy run off? Eddie decided he wanted to follow the guy; he had nothing better to do that day anyway.

He descended the squeaky ladder and walked back down the alley to the last spot he saw the man. He poked his head around the corner of the building to see if he was still there, trying to keep hidden in case the man was violent. The man in jeans was not close, but further down the street, walking alone. Quickly, the man jumped back toward the street, away from the building and spun around in a circle, as if he was spooked by something in the window of the store he was passing.

Eddie watched the man in jeans for a bit from around the corner of the building. The man appeared to just stand there looking back & forth, confused, then started walking down the street again, and turned another corner. Eddie came from around the building and jogged down the street to the spot where the mystery man started acting oddly. He could see nothing in the window or anywhere in the area that would cause that kind of reaction. Why was this guy acting so strangely? Perhaps he was an escaped mental patient?

Eddie decided it was best to just avoid this guy entirely, and find himself some breakfast. He walked backwards a little bit before turning around completely and heading down another street, away from the man and toward a shelter he knew of that gave out free food occasionally. His stomach was growling.

Chapter 7

Few things are as disconcerting as hearing disembodied laughter, unless of course you couple it with being alone in an entire city and having woken up next to a headless corpse. Upon hearing the laughter, Luke took off running down the street, not knowing where to go. The laughter was coming from every direction. Where would be safe? He covered his ears and continued running, hoping to escape the sound.

Turning the next corner onto a different street, he was struck in the head from above. He slowed his running and glanced back to see what it was. Immediately he noticed it was a dead black bird. Then another, and another, and then hundreds of them falling from the sky. More hit him on the head, shoulders, and arms. Even though they had soft bodies, they still hurt, and some of the claws and beaks cut his skin. He quickly ducked under the nearest awning and into a doorway of a building to get out of the death storm.

As he stood in the doorway watching the birds rain from above, he realized the laughter had stopped. Replacing the laughter now was the nauseating sound of thumping and glass breaking as the birds landed on every surface in the street. His current location was safe from falling objects, so he decided now would be a good time to rest while he decided what to do next.

He sat down and pulled out his cell phone. He tried to make some calls but they would not go through. Cursing at the screen, he furiously pressed the send button repeatedly but continued to be greeted with the same message every time. “No Service.” He finally gave up pressing the button and was about to put the phone away when he noticed an icon had just lit up on the top of the screen.

This was an icon he had seen many times before, three curved lines of increasing length, one over the other forming a cone shape. It meant there was a Wi-Fi signal available. This was great news for Luke. If there was an open Wi-Fi signal, he could make a call over the Internet. He went into network settings and found the signal was indeed available although its strength was weak. The name of the network, however, troubled him. The network was called “How did those birds feel?”

Clearly, he was not alone and he was being watched. He stared at the screen, wondering if he should connect to the network anyway and try making a call. He pressed connect and waited for confirmation. He was now successfully connected to the open Wi-Fi signal. Simultaneously, the dead birds ceased to fall. The storm was over. He stood up and walked out into the street. The birds were gone, none to be found anywhere. There was no shattered glass or other visible damage. The cuts on his arms and head were even missing.

"What the hell is going on," Luke said out loud.

His phone rang. The screen revealed "Answer me" as the name of the caller. No phone number was shown. He answered the call with a wary, "Hello?"

"What are you doing here?" asked the caller.

"Who is this?" asked Luke. "How did you get my number?"

"Did he send you to try and stop me?"

"What the hell is going on? Did who send me?"

"Either you are dumb, or you play dumb very well," said the caller.

"I just want to know where I am and how I got here," said Luke.

"You are exactly where you need to be," the caller said, then disconnected.

"Hello! What is going on," Luke screamed as he tried to redial the call. There was no number, so the call didn't go through.

"What do I do now?" asked Luke.

Obviously he was being watched, so the person behind the mysterious call and Wi-Fi signal must have been close by. He looked back down at his phone again and found that the signal was still there, weak but still present.

"If I can find the source of the signal, maybe I can find the guy on the phone, and perhaps a way out of here," said Luke.

He scrolled down though the list of apps on his phone. He found and opened the one called "Wi-Fi Analyzer" and began a scan.

Chapter 8

Joseph pulled away from the curb so quickly that the tires on his old Cadillac actually squealed for a couple of seconds. Tina put up the window as fast as she could, while letting out a nervous scream. She looked back toward the area where they had just been parked, but saw nothing except a cloud of dust left by the car's tires.

"That's it, I'm out of here. We're going home," said Joseph.

"Okay by me," replied Tina. "I'm so scared. What happened to everyone and what was that laughter?"

"Honey, I have no damn idea and I'm not sticking around to find out."

Joseph circled around the block to head back out of the city, but the road that would normally lead out was missing. He looked around at the street signs to make sure he was in the right area. There was even a sign saying "To Bridge" with an arrow pointing in the correct direction, but the road was gone. In its place now was a building that looked like it had always been there.

"What the hell? Where is the road? Where did that building come from, it wasn't there before, I'm sure of it," said Joseph. "This is the way we came in, isn't it?"

"Yeah Daddy, pretty sure," said Tina. "I don't know my way around as well as you, but I'm almost certain we came in this way. We only circled around the block. It's kinda hard to get lost doing that."

"Yeah. Well I'm going to try going down and over a few streets to try to get around this block… find another way to the bridge," said Joseph.

He turned the car right and drove a few streets back toward the location where they had been parked when they heard the laughter. When they approached the spot, they noticed another car was now parked there. As they got closer, both noted that it looked oddly like their Caddy; in fact, it was identical to their Caddy. It was the same year, color, convertible; even the license plate was the same. How could this be possible?

Joseph slowed his approach to get a better look at the car. As they rolled up next to the other Cadillac, they could tell that no one was inside. He came to a full stop next to the other vehicle and they both rose up in their seats to get a better look inside the other car's windows. Inside, they saw their duplicates, another Tina and Joseph, but dead. The car seats were covered in blood and the back seat was torn to shreds. On the passenger side window appeared to be a bloody handprint smeared down the inside of the glass.

Tina screamed. "Daddy, get us out of here!"

Joseph hit the gas pedal and drove away from his and Tina's corpses as fast as the car could take them. He was doing nearly seventy miles per hour when he noticed a woman in a white dress and hat with a stroller walking across the street up ahead.

"Look out," Tina yelled.

He slammed on the brakes, skidded a good distance, and turned the wheel sharply to the right. The car spun out of his control and side swiped another empty car, stalling out, breaking the windshield, and popping a tire on Tina's side.

The two of them sat in the wrecked car, crying and hugging each other. Over her father's shoulder, Tina could see in the direction where the woman had been walking. She was gone. There was no sign of her in sight, anywhere at all.

"Daddy, that lady with the stroller is gone," Tina said.

Joseph broke the hug and looked around. The woman was certainly nowhere to be seen. Down the street a little further, he noticed a giant flashing billboard, which read, "Just crashed your car? City empty? Can't find the way home? 110 4th Ave. We can help."

Chapter 9

The falling swarm of black birds seemed to go on for at least five minutes, and then almost as suddenly as it had begun, it stopped. He looked down at the street again with the binoculars, but he could not see any of the birds anywhere on the street. He lived fairly close to his company's building, so he decided to call over there to see if anyone else had seen the birds.

As he crossed his bedroom to get his phone off the nightstand, there was a knock on the door. He looked down at his watch, which read almost exactly nine o'clock.

"Who is it?" he asked.

The visitor responded with more knocking, louder this time, in the fashion of "shave and a haircut".

"Who is it," Jonathan repeated, almost shouting.

No one responded. He wondered who it could be. He didn't have any friends that would show up unannounced, especially at this time of day. He especially didn't know anyone who would respond to a "Who is it" question with a tacky knock like that.

He went out into the living area, walked up to the door, and gazed through the peephole. No one was there. It was just an empty corridor with a clear view of the elevator, which according to the readout, was on the first floor of the building.

He turned his back and began walking to his room again when the knocking came a third time. Quickly, he ran back to the door and looked through the peephole. This time he saw a baby on the floor, crawling back to the elevator doors, which were now open, but the there was no car inside. Realizing the baby was going to quite possibly fall into an open elevator shaft, he unlocked his door and ran out into the hallway.

By the time he got the door open and ran out, the baby was gone and the elevator doors were closed. According to the display, the elevator was still on the first floor. There was nowhere the baby could have gone. There were no other doors on this floor except his. Were his eyes playing tricks on him?

He approached the elevator and pushed the button. Nothing happened. He pushed the button several more times, each time harder and faster than the last. Still, nothing happened. The button never lit and he heard no sounds of a moving elevator inside. It was obviously broken, which would require a call to maintenance for repair, along with that other call to his office about the birds. This morning was shaping up to be quite an odd day, and Jonathan didn't care for oddness.

He turned and started walking back to his door and just when he was about to walk through, it slammed shut in his face. He stood in disbelief for a few seconds, and then tried to open it. It was locked. He realized that in his rush to save the mystery baby, he left his wallet and keys on his entryway table, inside his home. On an occasion like this, he would go down to the lobby and report the lockout to the maintenance department in person, but the elevator was also broken. Rather than descend twenty flights of stairs, he decided that he needed to get back in his home by himself.

He tried pounding on the door, rattling the handle, even hitting and kicking the door to bust it open. It seemed his door was very secure, which on any other day would have been very pleasing to him, except now when he was the one trying to break in to his own home.

Giving up for a moment and sitting down with his back to the door, he heard a knock come from inside his home. He quickly stood up and backed away from the door a few feet. Then there came another knock.

"Who iiissss iiitttt," a voice from inside said playfully.

Puzzled, Jonathan said "What do you mean, who is it? This is my damn house. Who are you?"

"Who is it," the voice from inside said again, followed by another single knock and the sound of giggling.

"My name is Jonathan and this is my home. Open up immediately."

The sound of rattling could be heard from the hallway, and then the door opened a crack. Without hesitation, Jonathan kicked the door, opening it forcibly enough that the doorknob made a hole in the wall behind it. He looked inside and could not hear or see anyone. When he walked through he expected to see someone lying on the ground, injured from the door being kicked into them. There was no one around.

When he first moved to the city, he was the victim of a burglary, so he had purchased himself a nice home defense weapon for future protection. He reached into the nearby closet and retrieved his Remington 12ga, loaded with 00 buckshot.

He went room by room, slowly, quietly, looking and listening for the intruder, but found no one. After several minutes of searching and finding nothing, he decided it was best to finally make those two calls and get the elevator fixed. He didn't imagine that anyone would be in a hurry to assist someone on the twentieth floor without a working elevator.

He sat down on the bed, finished putting his socks and shoes on, and dialed the office. No one answered, not even the voicemail. Something was going on, but he was unsure of what. Somebody should have answered the phone; the switchboard, or a secretary, if the voicemail was broken. Having his company functional was a top priority for him and not answering the phone was unacceptable. Someone had to be held accountable.

He ended the call, and began placing the second call to building maintenance to fix the elevator, and now his front door as well. Just as he was about to press the send button, he heard a bell chime from the hallway outside his door. He got up, walked out to the front door, and noticed the elevator door was open. The light inside the elevator flickered occasionally and soft music could be heard from the speakers. Apparently the maintenance department was already aware of the malfunction and had fixed it. This pleased Jonathan, as he loved efficiency.

He took this as an indication that it was a good time to leave and decided to head over to the office to see what was going on and why no one was answering the phones. Someone would probably need to be fired, but he had no obvious use for the weapon anymore. He put the shotgun back in the closet, closed his damaged door as best he could, and headed into the elevator.

Chapter 10

As Eddie walked down the street, he noticed that he was alone. Aside from the man in jeans that he had seen acting strangely earlier, he was completely alone. Now having reached his destination, he found the door of the shelter locked and the window gates also pulled down and locked. Evidently they had never opened this morning. Now where would he get food? His stomach growled.

"Time to start checking cans," he said to himself.

The city maintenance department was unusually on their game this morning, as nearly every can he checked was empty. He continued strolling down the street checking cans and dumpsters until he finally came across the jackpot. Someone had thrown out a small loaf of bread, still wrapped and uneaten.

"Must have been past the sell by date," he thought to himself as he voraciously devoured slice upon slice of dry white bread.

It wasn't the best tasting bread, but it was food and it sated his hunger for the time being.

Eddie was finishing up the last slice of bread when he noticed the sound of a car idling nearby. Throwing the empty bread bag back into the garbage can, he hurried over to the next cross street. At the next intersection, he realized that he was only a few feet away from the rear end of an old grey Cadillac, which was sitting curbside with two people inside. Snooping around the side of the building, he tried to get a good look at the two people to see what they were doing. It appeared to be a man and woman each holding up cell phones and having a discussion. A minute passed before the car pulled away from the curb and turned the corner.

Eddie watched as the car drove away. A moment later, just as he was about to head back to his cardboard home and start collecting his salvageables for the day, the car reappeared from around another corner further down the street. It stopped in the middle of the road and he could see the man looking around as if he was confused or lost. The woman in the passenger seat was pointing at different buildings and signs, and then they drove off back down the same street.

As they approached the spot where they had been parked when he first saw them, the car peeled out and took off heavily accelerating down the road. A few blocks away it suddenly skidded, spun out, and hit another parked car.

"Oh, shit, that is some crazy shit. What the hell are they doing?" Eddie asked himself.

Deciding to be a Good Samaritan, he started heading down the road toward where the car was crashed to see if they were all right. Before he could reach them, they both climbed out through the driver's side door. Once in the street they appeared to stare up at a building across the way for a few seconds, then crossed the street and walked away from the accident.

Eddie shouted, "Hey, are you guys okay? What happened? Do you need help? Where are you going? Yo! Do you two need help?"

They either couldn't hear him or just ignored him.

Not wanting to be a thief, but also really needing money, Eddie decided it would be in his best interest to check the vehicle and salvage what he could from the wreck. As he was searching the glove box, he heard a door open in a nearby building. He looked up and saw a businessman walking out going across the street.

"Oh hey, don't worry man, I was just checking this car for an owner's name so I could call the police," said Eddie. "I wasn't doing anything, I swear, it's cool."

The businessman ignored him. He didn't even turn his head toward him to acknowledge his presence. It was almost like he couldn't hear or see him. This didn't shock or surprise Eddie in the least. Since he had become homeless, he noticed people treated him differently and would go out of their way to avoid him. He believed this was because everyone assumed that talking to a homeless person would get you mugged or that you would have to deal with begging.

"Yo man, can you hear me? I'm talking to you, Mr. Important," Eddie said sarcastically.

The man just kept walking. Upon reaching the other side, he walked to the end of the block and crossed over the next street. When he was about half way into the crosswalk, a large booming rumble of thunder rattled the surrounding buildings. Mr.

Important, now with a hurried pace, finished crossing and took cover safely under an awning. After a brief pause, he went into the lobby of the adjacent building.

"Man, this day is crazy. I need a drink," said Eddie as he continued searching the vehicle for valuables.

After his search of the glove box and under the seats was complete, he had a grand total of sixty-seven cents, a pack of gum, and a cassette tape of Starland Vocal Band.

"What a complete waste of time," he muttered to himself.

When he stood up, he saw the strange man in jeans from earlier wandering down the street holding his cell phone in front of his face. He stopped in front of the same building that Mr. Important had just gone in to. The man in jeans looked up at the building, back down at his phone, then back at the building once again before walking inside.

Chapter 11

The elevator ride down the twenty floors was uneventful. The soft elevator music helped calm his nerves from the mysterious knocking and baby sighting only moments earlier. He thought perhaps he had been working too hard lately and his mind was playing tricks on him. He decided right then that later in the day after all this mess was sorted out, he would finally make that call to the travel agent he had been considering for years now. A Caribbean cruise was just what he needed, provided he could find a suitable person to cover for him while he was gone.

When the elevator doors opened, he stepped out and heard a crunch. He looked down, lifted his shoe, and found he had stepped on a small doll and crushed its little plastic head. He thought to himself that maybe this was the baby he had seen earlier, but dismissed it without a second thought. It couldn't have been. To begin with, it was only a doll. It was much smaller than the baby he had seen in the hallway upstairs. It also wasn't moving or crawling.

He kicked the doll aside and into a pile of garbage that had spilled out of the knocked over can next to the elevators.

"Someone needs to clean this mess up. This is completely unacceptable," said Jonathan. "Where is the janitor?"

He looked up in the direction of the front desk where the security guard would normally be sitting, which was when he noticed the lobby was in complete disarray. It was filthy and covered in thick dust. Cobwebs were stretched from the walls to the ceiling. It seemed like the place hadn't been cleaned in at least ten years, when just last night it had been immaculate.

He walked up to the desk, blew the dust off the silver bell on the countertop, and rang it several times. The chimes echoed through the empty lobby. Growing more irritated, he smashed down harder on the bell, ringing it louder.

"Hello?" he shouted. "Is someone attending this desk? Am I talking to myself?"

No one responded. He was obviously getting nowhere with this situation. He figured he would continue on to his office and place a call to the building manager from there once he had taken care of his office staffing problem.

He turned and walked toward the lobby doors. The lobby doors had also not been spared from the destruction done to this building last night. They were bent inward at the bottom and partially off the hinges while still remaining locked shut at the center. Several coarse black hairs were stuck to the metal edges. It appeared as if something had been forced between the two doors at the bottom, bending them apart. He turned the lock and pulled one side open.

Outside, the day was gloomy. No sun, overcast skies, and the look of an impending thunderstorm threated to make his brief walk to work much worse. Over to this left, he could see a bum robbing a car. He decided to just ignore the man and avoid a confrontation. Besides, he didn't want to get hit up for money. He despised beggars. He worked hard for his money, so why couldn't they?

He hurried across the street, walked down the block and across the next crosswalk. He barely made it under an awning as a loud rumble of thunder swept through the area. Still no rain, but he was now safely covered, so he no longer cared what the weather might soon bring.

Now in front of his office building, he approached the doors of the building and pulled. They did not budge. He pulled and pushed briefly a few more times, shaking the doors, but they were securely locked.

"Locked? During business hours?" he asked.

He peered through the glass and could see the lights were on but no one was behind the reception desk. Taking his wallet out of his back pocket, he flipped through it and found the card key. He swiped the card once to open the door, then immediately swiped again to keep it unlocked. He placed the card back in his wallet, returned the wallet to his pocket, then pulled open the doors and stepped through.

Just as it appeared from the outside, the lobby and all immediately visible areas were empty. He hurried over to the restroom, reserved for use by only the receptionist, and pounded on the door.

"Maria? Are you in there?" he asked. "You are not supposed to leave your desk unless you have someone covering for you. You know the rules."

When no one answered, he pushed the door open slightly and again said, "Maria! Are you okay in there?"

When his calls went unanswered, he pushed the door open all the way, hoping to not find her being sick or on the floor. Fortunately she was not in there, ill or injured, but she was also not at her desk.

Jonathan stood motionless for a few seconds, staring at her desk, while he tried to think of where she might have gone. Then he noticed that she left the computer logged in to the desktop and a Word document opened. He walked up to the monitor and skimmed over the contents of the open document. It consisted of a memorandum to employees about some new security protocols that would soon be enforced.

As he was reading the memo, the overhead lobby television turned on. He glanced up at it briefly as it was not unusual to play a welcome video announcement when a visitor entered the building; however, it was not playing anything and there was no visitor entering the building. Instead, the television began changing channels, each of which was a blank screen with no sound or video. The channels kept counting up, one after another, until it reached channel twenty-nine and stopped.

An unrecognized male voice came over the television speaker, "Welcome Mr. Koenig. We're glad you made it safely this morning given the unfortunate circumstances you've encountered. We are all waiting for you on floor eleven. Please come up. It is urgent."

Simultaneously, the television turned off and the elevator doors opened next to the reception desk. He quickly surveyed his surroundings to see if he was being watched. There could be no other explanation for this odd set of occurrences other than someone was pulling a prank on him.

Anxious to find out the reason for all of this and how they managed to pull off such an elaborate set up, he stepped inside the elevator and pressed the button for eleven. Just as the doors were almost closed, leaving a gap about one inch wide, he saw the lobby go completely dark.

Chapter 12

A loud clap of thunder struck overhead as Luke walked down the sidewalk holding his phone in front of him. He pressed the scan button every few seconds. The app would perform a quick scan with every press of the button, showing all available Wi-Fi signals and their corresponding strengths. There was only ever one signal showing as available, and eventually it disappeared.

"No, it's definitely the other way," Luke said to himself as he stopped, turned around, and began walking back the way from which he had just come. "And I'd better hurry up too before it starts raining. That's the last thing I need… walk around lost AND in wet clothes."

The next press of the scan button revealed that he was correct. The signal was definitely stronger this direction. He reached the next block and pressed the scan button once more. It showed the signal was still getting stronger, so he turned the block and walked down the next street.

Three more presses of the scan button finally revealed excellent signal strength. This, he thought, must be the source of the signal he had been searching for. He stopped walking for a moment and glanced up at the building to see where his search had finally ended. Building 110, "Koenig Development Systems," a sign advised him. The name sounded familiar to him, but he couldn't recall where he'd heard the name or if it was of any significance to him.

He looked back down at his phone and pressed scan again. The result was identical to the last scan. This had to be the location of the signal. If he went inside, he should be able to find the person who called him earlier. If he found the mystery man, hopefully he could find out what was going on and perhaps even how to get out of here and back home.

Luke put his forehead up against the glass of the door and covered the sides of his face with his hands to eliminate glare and allow him to better observe the inside. The lights were off and he could see there was no one at the reception desk. There was a faint glow from what was probably a screen, or monitor, coming from behind the desk. He pulled his head back away from the door and tugged gently on the door handle. It inched open, proving it was unlocked.

He tossed around the idea of entering in his head for a few seconds, weighing the pros and cons, before finally deciding to just go for it. He put his phone back into his jeans pocket, pulled open the door, and stepped into the lobby.

Once inside, he felt around on the wall next to the door, the usual place for light switches, but found none. Even though the lights were off, sufficient daylight was coming through the doors and windows, which allowed him to survey the surroundings.

The glow behind the desk was indeed a computer monitor that was left on by someone, evidently named Maria, who had been typing a memo to the employees about a new card swipe system that was to be installed. While nothing looked suspicious, he was eager to find the person behind his earlier phone call. He decided to move on and continue his search.

On the other side of the lobby, he noticed an escalator leading up to the next floor, which was lit up. Perhaps, he thought, his mystery man was up there. He stepped onto the escalator and began walking up. Five steps up, the motor groaned into life and the escalator started taking him back down to the lobby. He continued to climb, but the quicker the tried to ascend the steps, the quicker the motor ran to match his pace. His slow climb turned into an all-out run and he was able to get to the top, despite the escalator's best efforts to prevent him from doing so.

Once at the top, he hunched over to catch his breath. Now breathing heavily, he turned to look at the escalator, which immediately stopped moving and started in reverse, heading up toward him. Someone or something was trying to make it difficult for him to progress in his quest.

Finally catching his breath, he stood up and checked out the area. This floor was a complete wreck. It was laid out as one giant room. No offices, meeting rooms, or closets were visible. All the office furniture was knocked around. There were chairs lying on their backs. Desks were on their sides. Papers and folders were scattered all over the floor.

The center of the room was free from clutter, as if it was intentionally cleared out to make room for the one tiny beige garbage can sitting in the middle of it. It was silent, except for the escalator behind him and a slow tapping sound, coming from the vicinity of the garbage can.

He cautiously approached the garbage can, leaned over, and gazed down to see what was making the tapping noise. Inside was a collection of dark liquid, almost black. As he was leaning over the can, he felt something hit the back of his neck. He reached back and rubbed his neck; it felt wet. Holding his hand up in front of his face, he saw that it was covered in blood.

He panicked and grabbed a nearby paper off the floor in an attempt to wipe off the blood. The source of the tapping noise was obvious to him now; it was dripping from the ceiling. The garbage can was intentionally placed there to catch the drips. When he looked up at the ceiling, the sight horrified him. An entire drop ceiling tile was saturated in blood and was sagging from the weight of the liquid it contained. He didn't even want to know how the blood got up there, but he knew that it was a vast quantity if it could fill a garbage can and make a tile sag like that.

The sight of that much blood made him nauseous and he almost vomited. He backed away from the can, stood a chair back up, and sat down to collect himself. A few minutes had passed before he heard a noise coming from upstairs. It was a creaking noise, almost like something on casters, rolling across the floor above him. He stood up, went to the next escalator, and ran up before giving it a chance to fight him like the last one. It, instead, remained motionless.

At the top and now on the third floor, the lights were completely off. Luke couldn't see anything except the light from the floor below. He tried squinting but could barely make out anything but dark shadows. He knew he needed to find the light switch so he reached his arms out to his sides looking for a wall, but felt nothing. Then, he remembered he could use his cell phone light.

He pulled the phone out of his pocket and opened up the flashlight app once more. He pointed the phone's light to the left and right, back and forth, but the room was too dark. The darkness appeared to just be swallowing the light, not allowing it to reveal anything except more darkness.

As he was searching the darkness, something brushed against his shin. Startled, he screamed and kicked his feet frantically, hoping to connect with whatever it was. His sneakers encountered nothing but air.

Chapter 13

Eddie stood on the sidewalk next to the crashed Cadillac with a look of bewilderment. He wondered what was so special about that building. The only people he had seen so far that day were all going into the same place. Surely there must be an explanation or was he simply missing out on something great? He certainly didn't want to be the only one excluded. Pocketing his sixty-seven cent plunder and popping a stick of gum into his mouth, he strolled across the street to the building where everyone was had gone.

Once on the sidewalk in front of the building, he gazed around looking for clues as to why people would be heading there. A sign was taped to the inside of the glass door, which read "Community appreciation day. Free chicken and beer for everyone!"

"Damn, free food and booze, no wonder. I like this place," said Eddie. "I hope they don't hassle me. I could really use something to eat and a beer sounds great right now, with all this weird shit happening."

"Okay," he said while looking around for the name of the company. "Koenig Development Systems… whatever the hell that means. Lead the way to the free food!"

He pulled open the door to the lobby and casually walked inside.

Eddie didn't smell any food. He certainly didn't see any food. Was this some kind of joke? He didn't like jokes that included both the promise and withholding of food. He didn't find it funny and he was most definitely not laughing. He needed an explanation.

Against the wall near the elevators was the reception desk. Surely he could find someone there to help, but it appeared no one was around. He did, however, see a sign on the counter that resembled a small sandwich board containing a picture of a fried chicken wing and a can of beer.

"Oh, here we go. Let's see…" he said while walking closer to the sign.

"Community party. Free food and beer, today only. 11th floor café," read the sign.

"Oh man, this is gonna be great," exclaimed Eddie.

He quickly moved over to the elevators and pressed the call button. Soon, the bell made its ding noise and the doors opened. He jumped inside, spun around, and pressed the button labeled eleven.

"I hope they have some slaw too," he said. "I can't have chicken and beer without slaw. I may be homeless, but I'm not a savage."

He became giddy, filled with the idea of stuffing himself with tons of free food. As the elevator doors were closing, he heard an intense demented laughter coming from above the elevator's ceiling. He wanted to get back out, but the doors were closed too far to fit through, so he jammed his arm through the gap. It didn't stop them from closing and instead the doors closed tightly on his forearm.

"Aaahhhh," yelled Eddie as he pulled back, squeezing his arm through the doors.

"Ow, my arm," he said.

When he rolled up his sleeve, he could see the door had managed to break the skin causing it to bleed slightly. He furiously pressed buttons, at first just "Door Open", and then moving on to all of them, followed by the red emergency button. None of the buttons had any effect, and the elevator car began moving. Only a few seconds after starting, it screeched to a stop. The normal lights flickered and shut off which triggered the dim emergency lights to power on.

He remembered the phone that was usually hidden in the panel below the buttons. Throwing the little door open, he grabbed out the phone and began screaming obscenities into it, mostly out of fear and anger, but also in the hopes that someone would quickly come to his aid.

A voice came over the phone, "How can I help you, sir?"

Eddie screamed, "You have to get me out of this thing, it's haunted and tried to eat me."

"Don't be ridiculous, sir. Just sit tight and we'll have you out of there soon. In the meantime, try to relax."

"You relax. Get me out of this God damned thing," said Eddie.

“God damned? I’ll tell you what. I’ll let you out when I’m ready. How about that?”

Stunned, Eddie stood in silence. The voice on the phone was the person responsible for his arm being hurt. It had to be.

“I’m sorry. Could I please get out now? Please,” Eddie begged.

The voice on the other side just chuckled and then hung up.

“Hello? HELLO? Can someone help me here?” asked Eddie.

He hung the phone back up and sat down in the corner of the elevator in the fetal position, crying softly.

Chapter 14

Both Tina and Joseph had been walking the streets for several minutes before finally coming upon Fourth Avenue. A quick survey of the building numbers revealed that they were very close, probably within a block, of number 110. Another large crack of lightning overhead quickly turned into a sudden torrential downpour of rain. They both took off running for number 110 which they could now see was very short distance ahead.

Just as they managed to make it under the awning of the building, the rain changed to large balls of hail. Relieved that they had made it to cover just in time, they both let out a sigh.

"I think we are here, kiddo," said Joseph while looking at the sign. "110 4th Avenue, Koenig Development Systems. That sounds familiar."

"Yeah Daddy, this is where my interview today was supposed to be," replied Tina. "This is the business that Uncle Richie's friend owns."

"Right, I'll be damned. It's like we are supposed to be here, or something," said Joseph.

"This is too weird. We tried our best to avoid this place and yet here we are," said Tina.

"Spooky," they both said together.

They turned and stared into the lobby, then looked back at each other.

"Should we go in?" Tina asked.

"As much as I don't like this whole day so far, we certainly can't stand out here in this crappy weather," said Joseph.

"I agree," said Tina as she pulled open the door. "You first, Daddy."

"So that's how it's going to be, huh? Send the old man in first," he said.

He shook his head and cross the threshold.

Walking behind her father, Tina followed Joseph into the lobby. Once inside, they realized that this place was empty, just like the rest of the city. Together, they stood alone in the lobby of the building, scanning the surroundings, looking for signs of life. Behind a door next to the desk, they heard a toilet flush, followed by the tearing and crumpling of a paper towel.

Tina jumped behind her father and peeked out around his arm as the door slowly opened. Out walked a man dressed in overalls with unkempt, long curly hair. The three of them just stood silently for a few seconds, staring at each other.

"Hi. Can I help you folks?" asked the man in overalls.

"Maybe," replied Joseph. "We are looking for some help. We crashed our car a few blocks over and saw a sign that said someone in this building could help us out. Any idea what that means or where we go?"

"I'm just the janitor here, so I'm not exactly sure, but I bet the boss would know. He's up on eleven."

"Hey, excuse me, Mr - ," said Tina.

"Lou. Everyone calls me Lou. No Mister. Just Lou," said the janitor.

"Lou. Ok. Lou, do you know where everyone went? The whole city is, like, abandoned," said Tina.

"Right. There was no one around anywhere that we saw," added Joseph.

"No one was around at all, but you crashed your car? How did you manage that?" asked Lou.

"Oh never mind, my eyes were playing tricks on me. Forget it. Do you know where everyone is," replied Joseph.

"Can't say I know anything about any missing people. I've been here all night cleaning," said Lou. "Boss says that some VIPs are coming today and he wants to make a good impression on them. He wants this place spotless," explained Lou.

"Alright, I guess we'll head up to eleven and ask your boss if he can help us out. Maybe he knows what is going on. Thanks anyway Lou," said Joseph.

"No problem, sorry I couldn't help more," said Lou. "Oh, but if you are going to go up to eleven, I would suggest taking the service elevator in the back. These main ones have been acting funny."

Both Tina and Joseph just stared at him with a puzzled look on their faces.

"I'll show you where it is, follow me," said Lou.

They followed the janitor around across the lobby and through some hallways and into the back room where the service elevator was located.

"Crazy weather we are having today, huh," said Lou. "Ah, here you go, the service elevator. Just get in, press eleven. You're good to go."

"Yeah, sure is, thanks again, Lou," replied Joseph.

Tina and Joseph both stepped into the elevator and turned around to face the door. When they turned around, Lou was gone. They popped their heads out and looked around, but he was nowhere to be seen. Tina shrugged her shoulders at her father and pressed the button for eleven. The doors closed.

"Why did that janitor guy, Lou, say the weather was crazy," said Tina. "The only way he would have known the weather was bad was if he looked outside."

"Right. If he saw the weather, he sure as heck would have seen the lack of people out there," said Joseph. "Something doesn't add up with this guy."

A minute later, the elevator bell made a ding and the doors opened. Tina was the first to step out; however, as soon as she was through, the doors quickly shut and trapped Joseph inside.

"Daddy," she yelled.

Tina began repeatedly pressing the button to call the elevator, but to no avail. She could hear the elevator start moving, then immediately stop. The doors opened, revealing Joseph standing inside, but the elevator had moved down one half the height of the car.

The both of them tried pressing buttons, but the elevator did not respond to anything. He would have to climb out.

"Oh man, I don't like this at all," said Joseph. "This is something you always see in horror movies."

"Daddy, you have to climb out, you can't leave me out here alone," said Tina.

"Okay, but we do this fast, I mean, really fast," said Joseph. "I'll jump up and pull myself out, you try to hold the doors open. Ready?"

"Yes, ready. Go," said Tina as she leaned against one door trying to brace it open.

Joseph jumped, pulled himself up, and belly flopped on to the tile floor. He crawled out a bit when suddenly the elevator car dropped down a little more, trapping his right foot.

Tina screeched, fearing the worst.

"Shit," yelled Joseph. "Quick! Untie my shoe! Hurry!"

Tina scrambled to his foot and pulled at the laces as Joseph squirmed, managing to get his foot free, minus the shoe.

Once free, they stood up and hugged each other. The elevator doors opened, and the car came back up to the correct position. He wanted to get his shoe, but didn't want to go back inside that damned elevator. Instead of trying to retrieve it, he just kicked off his other shoe so he wouldn't be walking crooked. Almost as if the elevator knew it couldn't lure him back in, the doors closed.

They both now stood alongside the closed elevator door, staring at a ground floor lobby. To their left were a reception desk and a door marked as restroom.

"Impossible," said Joseph.

"This looks awfully familiar," said Tina.

"It should, this is the damn lobby where we saw Lou," replied Joseph. "How the hell did we come out of the main elevator on the first floor when we entered the service elevator and rode it up to eleven? It doesn't make any damn sense."

They both looked at each other, then around the room.

"The hell with this place, let's get out of here," said Joseph, as he took his daughter's hand and pulled her with him, making a mad dash for the exit back to the street.

Chapter 15

Something had just brushed against his leg. He didn't want to stick around to find out what it was, even though it felt small. Luke stumbled back, turned around, and made a mad dash back down the escalator to the floor below.

At the bottom of the escalator was something he had not noticed before. Bloody footprints were leading away from the center of the room where the garbage can sat. They headed around the escalator to the back of the room; right to a closed door.

He followed them back, pressed his ear up against the door, and listened carefully. He did not hear anyone or anything on the other side of the door. Slowly and quietly, he turned the knob. Once the knob was fully turned, he threw open the door, intent on surprising someone and not being caught off-guard himself.

The door slammed into a pile of boxes and a metal shelf filled with cleaning products. A man in overalls, holding a Playboy magazine, jumped up from a chair.

"Whoa! Damn, you scared me. Can I help you with something?" asked the man.

"Who are you and what happened to everyone?" asked Luke. "What's with all the blood out here?"

"First, my name is Lou," replied the man. "Second, I don't know what you are talking about. I have been here all night so I don't know anything about any missing people."

"Third," he added, "what blood are you talking about?"

"I'm talking about the blood out here in this room; the bloody footprints that led me to this door."

"I just cleaned that room only a few minutes ago and there was no blood."

"Well it's there now. Take a look for yourself."

Luke led Lou out into the room. The room was immaculate. Nothing misplaced, nothing overturned, and certainly no blood anywhere to be seen.

"Blood huh? Kid, I think you better see a doctor," said Lou.

"But – it was here. I saw it. It was a huge mess. There was blood all over the place, dripping into a bucket from the ceiling.

I almost slipped on it," said Luke. "I couldn't have imagined it. I couldn't. It was real."

"Listen, I have been here cleaning this building all night. Boss says a bunch of VIPs are coming today and I have to get this place spotless for their arrival," said Lou. "I haven't seen or heard anything unusual at all."

"Well, someone called me earlier from this building," said Luke.

"There is no one here yet, besides me and the boss. Perhaps you should go talk to him," said Lou. "He is on floor eleven. Just go on up. OH, but take the stairs. Elevators are having problems."

"Yeah, the boss is a good idea. I think I will do that," said Luke. "Which way are the stairs?"

Lou turned and pointed at another door along the back wall.

"Over there. That door there is the stairwell."

"Thanks, Lou."

"You're welcome. Hey, good luck with the boss," said Lou.

Luke turned, walked to the stairwell door, pushed it open and began ascending the stairs.

A few minutes of climbing and almost half way up to the eleventh floor, a thought occurred to him.

"I don't know anything about any missing people," said Luke. "I never said missing; I only asked what happened to everyone."

From many floors below, Luke heard a door creak open then slam shut. He stopped walking so he could listen quietly. He expected to hear someone approaching, footsteps or something else, but he heard nothing.

"Hello," called Luke. "Who is there? Is someone down there?"

He received no answer. Dismissing it as some kind of building settling or HVAC generated pressure change, he continued climbing. As he went, he occasionally kept looking down the center of the staircase over the railing to be sure he wasn't being followed.

He made it up one more floor before he noticed that the lights on the bottom of the stairwell had gone dark. He paused to look and the next set of lights went out too, followed by the next.

"Oh crap," said Luke.

His slow climb turned into a sprint up the stairs. The quicker he went, the quicker the lights below him went off. The darkness pursued him faster than he could run until eventually it caught up to him. A second before the lights went out, he reached the next landing and found a door labeled number nine. He charged through the door just as the stairwell completely succumbed to darkness.

Chapter 16

Approximately five minutes had passed from when Jonathan stepped into the elevator and pressed the button for floor eleven. He considered himself a patient man, but five minutes for a ten-floor trip in an elevator was absurd. Something was clearly wrong with this elevator.

Impatience got the best of him, and he began pressing buttons in a futile attempt to make the elevator go faster. First it was just button eleven, over and over, but quickly changed to any and all buttons. That seemed to do the trick. The elevator made its ding noise and the doors opened. The display indicated that he was now on floor six.

"One minute per floor," he said while looking at his watch. "Completely insane. That is way too slow. What is going on today? Everything is broken."

He stepped out of the elevator, which closed quickly and suddenly behind him.

All the employees jokingly referred to floor number six as the cubicle floor. This was where all the programmers sat plugging away at their computers for eight hours a day. He shuddered to think of what that must be like. He could never live without the spaciousness of his corner office, loaded with windows, natural light, and all his plants. In fact, his office was almost a greenhouse and he loved it that way. He had to hire someone whose sole duty was taking care of all his plants.

"Anyone here," he yelled.

He received no response, so he slowly walked around the perimeter of the room, looking into the cubicles as he passed each one by. Every one of them looked the same; computer, monitor, filing cabinet. Only minor differences set them apart, such as pictures of loved ones, cats, dogs, etc.

As he continued passing each cubicle, he noticed that every computer was on and logged in. The occasional cubicle had a radio playing music at a soft volume as to not disturb their neighbors but still break up the silence.

At the end of the row of cubicles, he saw that the door for the manager's office at the end was ajar. He approached the door and pushed it open slowly with his foot. Once the door was fully open, he saw a janitor sitting behind the manager's desk, staring out the window with his back to the door.

Calmly, as if he sensed his approach, the janitor asked him, "Damn crazy weather we're having, huh?"

"What are you doing in here?" asked Jonathan.

"I'm on my break, saw the empty room, and thought no one would mind if I relaxed a bit," said the janitor. "I've been here all night cleaning. The boss says some VIPs are coming today and the place needs to be spotless."

"I'm the boss here, and I don't know you," said Jonathan.

The janitor spun the chair around to face Jonathan.

"Indeed, you are the big head boss, but you are not the one I was referring to," said the janitor. "Guys down on the bottom of the totem pole like me end up with several bosses. I'm a new hire this week, name's Lou. Everyone calls me Lou. New guy gets stuck cleaning all night while everyone else is home in bed. Isn't that how it always is?"

"Well, get out of this office, Lou, it belongs to the department supervisor and he wouldn't want you in here," said Jonathan.

"No problem, boss."

"Speaking of which, have you seen him, or anyone else around here?" asked Jonathan.

"No, boss, just you."

"Someone told me I had to go to floor eleven; that people were expecting me," said Jonathan. "Any idea what that is all about?"

"No, boss, no one on eleven that I know of. Last I checked, it was empty and I'm the only one here, well, besides you," said Lou. "What are you doing on six anyway?"

"Oh, the freaking elevator wasn't working properly. It opened here."

"Yeah, they've been having issues last night and this morning," said Lou. "If you are going to eleven, I would suggest taking the service elevator or the stairs instead."

"No kidding," said Jonathan. "Perhaps you should put up a sign saying they are out of order before someone gets stuck in them."

"Point taken, boss. Will do."

Lou stood up and walked around the desk to Jonathan. The two of them left the office. Jonathan locked the door from inside, closing it behind them.

"Oh, and call the elevator company to fix them at once," said Jonathan.

"Right on it, boss."

Lou turned and walked away from Jonathan, back to the front of the room toward the main elevators. Jonathan watched him walk away, then turned and walked toward the service elevators. A few steps away, he heard the office door open and close behind him.

"Hey, I told you to stay out of that office, you idiot," shouted Jonathan. "Don't you listen?"

Jonathan hurried back to the supervisor's office door and threw it open, expecting to see the janitor back in there behind the desk. Instead, a small black hairy creature popped out from behind the trashcan and brushed past his shin on the way out the door. It scurried down the hallway, around a row of cubicles, and out of sight.

Chapter 17

Drying his tears with his sleeve, Eddie just sat on the floor and rocked slowly, back and forth.

"Has the grown man finished crying now?" asked the voice on the speaker system.

Eddie lifted his head up and looked directly at the camera hanging in the corner of the ceiling.

"What do you want? Why won't you let me out?" asked Eddie.

"It's not what I want, so much as what the boss wants," said the voice. "He says you are a very important person and he would like to speak with you."

"Important? Important how? I don't get -"

"Don't be concerned with that now. All will be revealed when the time is right. I was just having some fun," said the voice. "I was bored because I have been alone here all night. If you are done crying, come on up to floor eleven."

The lights in the elevator car came back on to normal brightness.

"Eleven? The floor with the free food?" asked Eddie.

"Yes, Eddie, the floor with the free food. Don't keep him waiting," said the voice.

The elevator doors opened. Eddie pressed button eleven, but the button did not light up, nor did the doors close. He had to either get off on this floor or stay inside the elevator and risk being trapped again. After briefly considering his options, he stepped out onto the fourth floor. As soon as he crossed out into the room, the elevator doors shut quickly behind him.

"Shit shit shit," Eddie said as he repeated pressed the button, trying to get the doors to open again.

Giving up, he turned around and put his back against the wall.

Floor number four contained a meeting room. Directly in front of the elevator was a glass wall, separating the conference room table from the elevator, no doubt to provide a bit of privacy. He could see through the glass, and in the center of the conference room table was a bowl full of fruit. Waiting upstairs was free food, but he was hungry now and he didn't know how long it would take to get up to eleven without using the elevator. He badly wanted a snack.

He pulled open the conference room door and approached the table. He could clearly see that the bowl was filled with apples, oranges, bananas, and grapes. Now standing on the side of the table closest to the bowl, he reached out and grabbed an apple.

Just as he was about to take a bite, an oddly shaped black thing fell from the ceiling and onto the far end of the table. It was some sort of creature, not much bigger than a cat, but definitely not any kind of cat he had ever seen. It stood on four legs, scurried across the table, and jumped onto his chest. Its back legs had sharp claws that latched into his skin, much like a cat. Its front legs also had sharp claws, which slashed and scraped at his face, throat, and chest.

Eddie screamed and stumbled around the room, bumping into the furniture and walls. He pulled at the black thing by the back of its neck and was able to stop it from clawing him. The creature then turned its head completely around backwards, like it was possessed, and bit his wrist.

He screamed once more and dropped the creature. It landed on the floor with almost no noise at all. It jumped onto the table, then leapt up to the ceiling and crawled away into the ductwork, leaving Eddie bleeding on the floor.

Grabbing some tissues from a nearby box, he wiped his face of the blood. Behind the glass door, he heard the elevator ding and the doors open. When he turned to look, out walked a janitor pushing a bucket and mop, whistling. It didn't appear the janitor had seen him, as he began mopping up the floor around the elevator, and then backed into the glass door, pushing it open with his rear end.

"Yo, hey," said Eddie. "I need a little help over here."

The janitor turned and made the "whoa" whistle noise loudly.

"What happened here?" asked the janitor.

"Somcthing attacked me, clawed me up and bit me real good."

“Nah, nothing around here but the occasional roach or mouse,” said the janitor. “But whatever happened, you need to file an accident report with the boss.”

The janitor picked up a towel off his cart and tossed it to Eddie.

“He is up on the eleventh floor.”

Eddie wiped his face and chest with the towel, which had an odd smell to it, like cleaners or some kind of chemical.

“Funny you mention eleven. That’s where I was going,” said Eddie.

“Then what the blazes are you doing here on four? You’re a bit off,” said the janitor.

“Sort of a long story,” said Eddie. “…. Say, you guys have a doctor in this place, I suddenly don’t feel -”

Before he could get out his last words, he collapsed on the floor. He was not unconscious and could see what was going on, but couldn’t move or speak. Through blurry vision, he watched as the janitor put down his mop, grabbed his feet, and dragged him across the room.

He heard a ding and elevator doors opening, but from his view, all he saw was blurry ceiling. He felt himself being dragged again and finally saw that he was now in the elevator. The janitor stepped over him and left the elevator. He saw the janitor lean in and press the button for eleven.

“Good luck up there, buddy,” said the janitor. “Tell ‘em Lou sends his regards.”

The janitor just grinned as the doors closed.

Chapter 18

Joseph and Tina were half way across the lobby, heading towards the doors leading back to the street, when the lobby lights suddenly went dark. They both slowed to a walk, now only having a little daylight coming from the glass in the lobby to see where they were going. Cautiously, they continued to make their way to the exit. Joseph stumbled as his foot kicked into an object on the floor. He dropped Tina's hand in order to catch himself from falling.

Once he regained his footing, he said to her, "It's okay. It was just a fallen chair. Lets keep going."

Tina was now in front of her father. She reached back to grab his hand, but it was not there. She moved her arm around, searching for him, but found nothing. Just before she could turn around to find him, she heard a muffled scream from behind her. Even though the sound was muffled, she recognized it instantly to be the voice of her father, Joseph.

Tina spun around quickly and screamed out, "Daddy!"

Squinting to hopefully see better in the dim light, she saw a hooded shadow figure dragging Joseph, kicking and fighting, into one of the nearby elevators. Even though her father had at least forty pounds and a foot of height on the hooded figure, he was unable to break free. The figure reached over and pressed a button inside the elevator, and the doors began to close.

Tina again screamed for her father and ran as fast as she could towards the closing elevator doors. She was unsure what she would be able to do if she did manage to get there in time. Clearly the shadow figure was much stronger than her father, so she, too, would also be no match for him. Just before she reached the elevator, the doors fully shut. Her running came to an instant stop as she nearly ran face first into the doors.

She pounded on the doors, screaming, "Daddy," through tears.

A few seconds later she heard her father scream, "Run Kiddo, get out of here! Go find help!"

She didn't want to leave him behind. She thought that even if she could find her way out of the city, she had no car to do it. Her cell phone still had no signal and she had apparently no way of finding help or getting to it. Rescuing him was her only option, regardless of his wish for her to leave him and get out. She needed to find him and save him and up was the only direction to go. Resigning herself to saving him, she reluctantly reached over and pressed the elevator call button.

The second elevator's doors opened nearly instantly. She knew she had no idea what floor her father was taken to, so instead of getting in and guessing, she had the brilliant idea to just wait a minute to see where the other elevator stopped. Bringing her tears under control, she waited and watched the digital screen beside the elevator her father was dragged in to. Eventually the numbers stopped changing when the display read nine. She nervously stepped in to the elevator, pressed nine, and watched the doors close.

After a short wait, the elevator chimed and the doors opened on the ninth floor. This floor was a giant empty room. She looked around for signs that her father was here, but found absolutely nothing. The room was completely empty, not even a speck of dirt to be seen. She looked back at the elevator screen on the wall, and the other elevator now indicated it was on eleven, not nine. Perhaps it was not done moving or it had made a quick stop here for some other reason? Regardless, she now knew she had to go up to eleven.

She stepped back in the elevator and pressed the button for eleven. She was looking down at her feet as the doors closed, when she heard a man's voice yell out "Hey!" By the time she looked back up to see the source, the doors had fully closed.

Chapter 19

Luke burst out of the stairwell onto the ninth floor and slammed the door shut behind him. Unsure of what was following or chasing him, he leaned back against the door and braced it to help keep it shut. Pushing on the door, he listened for noises of someone coming up the stairs. He heard nothing from behind the door.

After about a minute of pressing against the door, he finally eased up and looked around to survey his surroundings. The large room was completely empty, but across the way he could see the elevators. One of them was open and he saw a woman inside. The doors began closing and Luke yelled out "Hey," to hopefully catch her attention. She either didn't hear him, or didn't care, because she allowed the doors to close with no verbal or physical response to his call.

Luke again yelled, "Hey," as he ran over to the elevators to attempt to catch her.

When he reached the elevator wall, he pressed both up and down buttons. The other elevator opened shortly after, indicating it was going up. The display on the elevator the woman left in was indicating it was on floor ten.

Luke pulled his cell phone out of his pocket and once more fired up the app that allowed him to check the Wi-Fi signal strength in the area. It did a quick scan and showed that the signal he had been following earlier in the day was indeed still present and of excellent strength.

It appeared that his only hope of getting out of this place and back home again was to continue on his quest to find the person responsible for the Wi-Fi signal, and his mysterious phone call earlier. According to the janitor he met, that person was up on floor eleven, so that was where he needed to go. He looked over at the display on the elevator where the woman was, and that indicated it was now on eleven, not ten. Was that some kind of weird coincidence? Everything was leading him to this place and floor eleven.

Luke walked back over to the stairwell and listened again for the sound of someone on the other side. He still heard nothing. He reached down and grabbed the doorknob and turned it slowly and quietly, but it was locked. He pressed harder, but it still would not turn.

"Damn," said Luke. "I guess I have to take the elevator now."

He remembered his earlier conversation with the janitor, who told him to avoid the elevators, but he looked around the empty room and there was no other way. He would have to take the elevator up to eleven. He began heading back over to the opposite wall.

Two steps from the stairwell door, he heard the knob rattle. There was nowhere to hide, so he ran over to the corner of the room on the same side as the stairwell door and pressed himself up in the corner as close as he could get. Hiding in plain sight was something children usually did while playing hide and seek, but he had no other choice at this moment.

The door creaked open and he saw a small black creature come through the doorway. A foot into the room, it paused, looked up, and appeared to be sniffing the air. A few seconds later, it ran across the room and jumped up to the ceiling, knocking loose a ceiling tile. It jumped again, up through the now open hole and climbed out of sight.

Luke let out a deep sigh. He snuck out a bit more into the room and looked back toward the door. It was still open from when the creature entered. Now was his chance to get out of here. He hurried as quietly as he could back to the door and entered the stairwell. All the lights were back on again and it was well lit. To prevent the creature from following him, he closed the stairwell door behind him.

Chapter 20

Jonathan had never seen anything even slightly resembling that black creature. It was definitely not any kind of cat or dog that he had ever seen. It was sort of shaped like a ball that was being pressed down; round but slightly oblong, and covered in coarse black hair, blacker than anything he had ever seen before. The hair was so dark that it appeared to almost consume light.

Freaked out by the presence and very nature of this creature, he hurried back to the service elevators that Lou had suggested he use. The doors to the elevator were already open, so he stepped inside and pressed the button for floor eleven. Around the corner, the black creature appeared. It stopped and just watched Jonathan standing inside the elevator. Jonathan noticed this and became nervous at its behavior. Its eyes seemed to be red, but not solid, swirling. It looked hostile and Jonathan wanted to avoid all future contact with it, starting right then. He reached over and pressed the eleven button again, and again, and a few more times, including the door close button for good measure.

The doors finally began to close, and the creature seemed to notice its prey was going to get away. It immediately began a full speed gallop like motion toward the elevator. Just as the doors fully shut, there was a loud bang noise, followed by scratching and growling sounds, growing more distant as the elevator continued up. After a few more seconds, the creature's noise was gone and the only sound Jonathan could still hear was his own heavy breathing.

"What in God's name was that thing?" Jonathan asked himself.

About another minute of a completely uneventful ride passed before the elevator finally stopped. The display read eleven, then chimed, and the doors to floor eleven opened.

Jonathan stepped out and immediately noticed a man lying on the floor in the center of the room.

"Hey! Buddy," Jonathan called out. "Are you okay?"

There was no answer from the man. He appeared to be either dead or unconscious. From the amount of cuts and bruises the man was covered with, and the blood present on his clothing, Jonathan guessed the former and that the man was in fact dead.

Not liking to assume anything, he walked up to the man, intending to search for a pulse.

"Ah. VIP number two has arrived," said a deep voice behind him.

Chapter 21

Quickly, Tina began mashing the door open button, but it was already too late. The elevator had begun moving up toward the eleventh floor. She wondered whom it was that yelled out to her as the doors were closing. She hadn't seen anyone else besides her father and that weird janitor all day. It didn't sound like either of those two, so she was a bit hopeful knowing that someone else was there.

The ride up went very quickly. The elevator chimed and opened, not on the eleventh floor, but the tenth. Sitting on a chair immediately outside the elevator doors was her father.

"Daddy," Tina yelled as she ran out to him.

Joseph grabbed her and they hugged for a few seconds without saying a word.

"What took you so long, Kiddo?" asked Joseph.

"I was on the way to where I thought you went, and I heard a voice yell out to me," said Tina. "I didn't see who it was, but there is someone else here. Maybe they can help."

"I don't know. I am inclined to not trust anyone or anything I see at this point. I expect you to do the same. There has been way too much strange stuff going on today."

"What happened to you anyway?" asked Tina. "I saw a hooded guy drag you off into the elevator. I didn't expect to find you so easily."

"Truth be told, I thought I was a goner. The guy had me in a choke hold the whole elevator ride," said Joseph. "He was super strong; could have broken my neck but didn't."

"Well I'm glad he didn't," replied Tina.

"Me too, Kiddo," said Joseph. "When we got out on this floor, he pointed to this chair and let me go. I figured he meant I should sit since he didn't say anything. I sat down then he got back in the elevator and left. That's all I know."

"Well I didn't see him on my way up, he must have been in the other elevator car," said Tina.

"Probably," replied Joseph. "After he left I pressed the buttons and nothing happened so I sat back down and just waited. There is no other way out of this little room besides this elevator, so I didn't have much of a choice."

"Well the elevator seems to be working fine, so lets get out of here," said Tina.

"I don't think that is the best move at this point in time," said Joseph. "It looks like someone is trying to prevent us from leaving and is intending us to go up to the eleventh floor. I think if we try to escape again, we will fail. Maybe next time we don't end up so lucky."

"So what, continue up to eleven?" asked Tina.

"Exactly," said Joseph. "I think we have to."

The two of them entered the open elevator car and reluctantly pressed button eleven. As the doors closed, they gave each other a nervous glance. Each one knew what the other was thinking; they worried about what they might find on floor eleven. They didn't have much time to worry. The elevator door opened almost as quickly as it had closed. The trip up to the last floor was near instant.

As soon as they stepped out of the elevator, they realized they were not alone. Present in the room were three men, none of whom looked familiar to either Tina or Joseph. One man was lying on the floor. The second man was standing over the man on the floor; he was sharply dressed in an expensive looking business suit.

"Excellent. VIP numbers three and four have also arrived," said the third man, from his seat behind a desk in the corner of the room. He was also dressed very well, in a dark suit. He had jet-black hair and didn't look up when speaking. He appeared to be referencing a tablet in his hands.

Chapter 22

As Luke ascended the remaining flights of stairs, he continually looked down over the railing, checking for movement, seeing if he was being followed. The first few steps were uneventful, which helped calm his nerves. There were only two floors to go, so he had no need to rush at that point. He felt it was best to conserve his energy for when he reached the eleventh floor and whatever might be waiting for him there.

He had reached the top of the current set of stairs when he heard footsteps below. He leaned over the railing and looked down to see who was following him. What he saw was a hooded shadow figure a few floors below. Luke gasped. It was the same hooded figure he had seen in the window when he was walking down the street earlier in the day, he was certain of it. They exchanged a long stare, when finally the shadow figure broke the gaze and began climbing the steps at an alarming rate.

Luke took off running as fast as he could, skipping every other step. When he reached the tenth floor, he stopped and yanked on the door. It was locked and would not budge. He looked down over the railing again. The hooded figure was still ascending the stairs, and catching up quickly. It seemed like for every two steps Luke was able to climb, the hooded figure was able to do ten.

Giving up on the locked door, Luke continued to run up the stairs two at a time. When he finally reached the door marked as eleven, he leaned over one last time to see where the hooded figure was. It was only one set of stairs below him at this point. Terrified, he grabbed the knob, slammed the door open, and charged into the room at full speed.

He now stood in the middle of an office like room, surrounded by other people. These were the only other people he had seen since waking up in the mysterious alley room that morning, except for the janitor. On the floor was a dirty, bleeding, older man, who seemed unconscious. Standing over him was another man in a business suit. Past these two, near the elevators, were two more people. One was an attractive younger woman, probably close to his age. The other was an older man.

Judging by the way she was clinging to him, he was probably her father.

As he stood there staring at these people, a voice came from the corner of the room behind him.

"Ah, the late addition. More are always welcome."

Luke turned to look in the direction of the voice.

"Is that man dead?" asked Luke, pointing down at Eddie.

"Good question. I was just about to check for a pulse," added Jonathan.

"You really don't know, do you?" asked the man behind the desk, still looking down at his tablet. "How ironic."

Jonathan knelt down next to the man and felt his neck for a pulse.

"So? Is he dead?" asked Joseph.

"He seems to only be unconscious. I found a pulse," said Jonathan, turning to look at the man behind the desk. "What are all these people doing here in my office, and who the hell are you?"

Before the man could answer, Eddie let out a moan and opened his eyes. He had to squint a bit to see because of the suddenly bright lights he was exposed to, but he saw a man standing over him and a bunch of other people around him. He couldn't be sure, but they all looked familiar.

He rolled over and pushed himself up to a standing position. He had a really bad headache and his arm still hurt. Standing there, rubbing his arm and head, he recognized the others as the people he had seen earlier in the day. Mr. Important, the two people in the car, the man in jeans from the alley - they were all here.

"I know you people. I saw you all earlier today out in the streets acting weird," said Eddie. "Why are we all here? What's going on?"

"Thanks for finally joining the party, Eddie," said a man sitting behind a desk.

Chapter 23

The man behind the desk finally put down his tablet and got up. He was a very intimidating specimen. He stood about six feet six inches tall and wore a dark charcoal grey Italian three-piece suit. His hair was shiny and black with a few streaks of grey at the temples. He appeared very well built and muscular, with broad shoulders and a thick neck. By all appearances, this man could have been a professional wrestler or football player.

"It appears everyone is here, so we can finally get started," said the man.

The man behind the desk clapped his hands three times very loudly. Immediately, the door to the stairwell opened. The hooded shadow figure walked out into the room, and approached the desk where the man stood. From his pocket, he retrieved a small object that resembled a snow globe, which he then placed on the desk next to the man. Turning to face the people in the room, he removed his hood and grinned.

Simultaneously, everyone in the room gasped.

Facing the man behind the desk, Jonathan stepped forward and asked, "You haven't answered my question. Who are you and what are these people doing in my building?"

The man responded, "Today, this is my building and this is my office." Indicating to the formerly hooded figure, he said, "I trust you all have met Lou."

Everyone stood speechless and stared as Lou walked over to the stairwell door and pulled it open a few inches. Out scurried the black creature, which walked over to the desk and jumped onto it, sitting down next to the snow globe like object that Lou had placed there.

Eddie screamed and ducked behind Jonathan, who was the closest person to him at the time.

"Keep it away from me," Eddie yelled. "That thing did this to me. It attacked me."

"Now, now. Calm yourself, Eddie," said the man standing behind the desk. This is my pet. Don't you like him? I made him myself."

"What the hell is that thing?" asked Luke. "And what do you mean, you made him yourself."

"Oh, he is nothing in particular. I had a lot of inspiration from various species of animals. He is primarily Tasmanian Devil, mixed with a few other animals' characteristics," said the man.

"But, how can you create him yourself? Are you some kind of genetic engineer or something?" asked Joseph.

"Nothing of the sort. I just happen to be a man of several talents," said the man. "Obviously, none of which are manners. Excuse me. Allow me introduce myself. My name is Nate," he said with a slight bow.

"Why don't you tell them the best part, Sir," added Lou.

"As you all can see, Lou here gets impatient when he is excited. It's one of his flaws. If he wasn't so good at his job, I would not have tolerated it for so long," said Nate.

Nate chuckled and paused for a moment, pulling a cigar out of his inside jacket pocket.

"Allow me to appease Lou and tell you all the best part," said Nate. "You are all dead."

Chapter 24

Everyone present, upon hearing the ridiculous statement made by Nate, just stood silent. The first one to break the silence was Tina, who hadn't said anything since everyone had gathered in the room.

"What do you mean, we are all dead?" asked Tina.

"Yeah, what do you mean," added Joseph.

"I mean, simply put, none of you are alive," said Nate. "What do you think 'dead' means?"

"Perhaps I don't understand," said Jonathan. "Are you speaking metaphorically, because I am clearly not dead."

"Rest assured, Mr. Koenig, you are deceased," responded Nate. "Allow me to explain."

Nate pointed his finger at Eddie.

"You, Eddie, what do you remember before waking up this morning?" Nate asked.

"I'm not sure. I was sitting in my box, playing solitaire. I heard a loud noise. Then, this morning, I saw that kid over there climbing down a fire escape," said Eddie, pointing toward Luke.

Nate now pointed his finger at Jonathan.

"And you, Mr. Koenig, what do you last remember?"

"I got home from a particularly bad day at the office. I ate a quick meal and had a drink," said Jonathan. "Then I woke up in bed this morning. I assumed I had too much to drink and just didn't remember going to bed."

"I'm sure the rest of you have similar experiences with missing time. This is my point," said Nate. "What I am doing here is the Devil's work. I am his right hand man, if you will. You see, he gives me a list," he explained, indicating to the tablet on the desk. "I don't question why people are on the list, they just are. You must have grabbed his attention in some way. Anyway, I take this list, and my associates and I gather their souls for the boss. We do, however, get to have some fun in the process."

"Come on, this is complete bullshit," said Joseph. "Do you expect us to believe this crap?"

Nate calmly walked over to Joseph and grabbed him by the throat with this left hand. Without any effort at all, he lifted him off the ground and squeezed.

"Stop it! Stop! Daddy," yelled Tina. "What do you want from us?"

Still holding Joseph in the air, Nate responded, "I already told you dear. I want your souls."

With his right hand, he retrieved a long blade from his jacket pocket. In one smooth motion he lopped the head clean off Joseph and let his body fall lifeless to the floor.

Everyone screamed. Tina began crying.

"Shut up. All of you," said Nate. "Screaming and crying will get you nowhere."

Still holding the severed head of Joseph, Nate turned and nodded at Lou. Lou approached Nate and took the head in both of his hands, squeezing it until it became smaller and eventually disappeared. When he opened his hands, the head was gone and floating in its place was a small puff of lightly colored blue vapor.

Nate walked up to the desk and picked up the snow globe object. He carried it over to the floating blue cloud and touched the two together. The blue cloud was sucked into the globe. He approached the group of people and held up the globe. Inside was Joseph, banging on the wall of the glass object, silently screaming.

"Now do we believe?" asked Nate. "The boss likes to keep them safely in these things. He calls them his keepsakes. He puts these on shelves for display, sort of like souvenirs. Each one tells a story."

Screams and crying once again filled the room.

"Answer me this," yelled Nate over the screams. "Why is it that none of you remember going to sleep last night? It is because you all died last night. This place is limbo."

"Now, remember how I told you we like having fun while doing our jobs?" asked Nate. "Well, we play tricks on people. Torture them mentally before finishing them off. It's always groups of people too. You're probably heard about our work, read it in the paper or saw reports on the TV news, and just never even realized it. Groups of people all die the same way," he said.

"So you brought us all here to kill us?" asked Jonathan.

"Wrong again, Mr. Koenig," said Nate. "I brought you all here to torture you before collecting you. As I said earlier, you are already dead."

Nate looked around the room.

"So who wants to be next? Any volunteers?"

Chapter 25

The group of people now huddled together in the center of the room.

"Solidarity is cute, but pointless," said Nate.

Nate approached the group and punched Eddie square in the stomach, dropping him to the ground.

"Come take care of this man," said Nate, motioning to Lou.

Lou approached Eddie, stepped on his chest, and grabbed him around the neck. Simultaneously pulling and twisting, he ripped off Eddie's head with almost no effort. Then, in a similar fashion to Joseph, he squeezed it very hard until it was no longer visible. A puff of blue vapor now hovered in the room. Just as before, Nate walked up to it with the same keepsake and it was sucked in. Inside the keepsake now stood Joseph and Eddie, both banging on the glass.

"Now you, Miss. What do you remember?" asked Nate.

"I don't… I can't…" she said softly as she wept.

"Come now, surely you remember rehearsing your interview questions."

"Yes, I do… but that's all. Then I woke up and here we are."

Nate circled the group.

"Such a pretty thing. It's a shame you'll have to witness another person die in front of you," said Nate, who then snapped his fingers and whistled.

The black creature jumped down off the desk and scurried across the room. It ran up to Jonathan and bit him in the calf, causing him to fall to his knees with a scream. Nate grabbed him by the hair and sliced across his neck. The screaming stopped. His body fell to the ground with a thud. He then tossed the head over to Lou, who squeezed it out of existence and into a cloud of vapor that was immediately collected by the keepsake.

Luke and Tina both hugged each other tightly while crying.

"I told you solidarity would do you no good," said Nate.

Suddenly, Tina broke the embrace and ran for the stairwell door.

Lou let out a large intense laughter and said, "They always resist. I like watching them try to get away."

When she reached the door, she pulled as hard as she could, but it would not budge. Lou walked up behind her and slammed her face into the door, then threw her on the ground. Nate approached her and kneeled down.

"Oh, when I said you were pretty, I meant it. Too bad Lou had to mess it up."

He took his knife and stabbed her in the chest while covering her mouth. With a twist, he withdrew the blade and stabbed her in the throat. She became limp and stopped resisting. Lou picked her up and in the same fashion as the others, squeezed her head until the vapor appeared. Nate held out the keepsake and watched as the vapor was sucked in.

Holding it in front of his face, he said, "Four down. Almost done. Now we just need to clean up this late entry."

They both looked at Luke, who stood there in disbelief at what had just taken place.

"Has anyone ever escaped?" asked Luke.

"Never," replied Nate.

"Do you expect me to just give up?" asked Luke.

"No one has ever just surrendered themselves," said Nate.

Luke surveyed the room for possible escape options. The only exits were the elevator, which would take too long, and the stairs, which he knew were locked based on Tina's attempt. Then a thought occurred to him.

"I never said anything about surrender," said Luke, as he took off running across the room.

He ran full speed, straight at the desk in the corner of the room, jumped onto the surface, and leapt at the window. A split second before he hit, he turned his back to the glass, tucked his head, and covered his face.

"Fool! Suicide will not prevent us from collecting you," yelled Nate.

With a large bang and shattering sound, Luke crashed through the glass.

Both Nate and Lou walked up to the shattered window and watched as Luke plummeted to the ground.

"Go down and scrape up the carcass," said Nate. "Bring it back to me so we can fin-"

Nate cut himself off in mid-sentence. He was watching Luke fall, but just as he was about to witness the satisfying splat, he vanished. No splat. No bloody mess on the sidewalk. No satisfaction.

Chapter 26

He woke up screaming, kicking his legs and swinging his arms. It felt like he was falling. Quickly realizing that he was safe in bed, he calmed down, reached over to the lamp, and turned it on.

"Oh, thank God! I'm home," he exclaimed. "What the hell was that? A dream?"

In all the years since he had begun having the blackouts, never had one seemed so real. Never had he been able to remember a dream so vividly. He just sat in bed, staring at the wall. It all seemed so real.

He looked out the window and saw that the sun was finally coming up. It was dawn. He decided to go for a nice run. The cool, crisp, morning air would do him well. He ate a quick meal, got dressed, and headed out.

An hour later, he came home feeling refreshed. He picked up the newspaper from his doorstep and went in for a shower and breakfast. The entire time he was in the shower, all he could think about was that dream. He decided that after his shower, he would Google some names he remembered from the dream. He quickly finished showering, got dressed, and headed back to the kitchen.

He sat down at the table. As he unfolded the newspaper, his jaw nearly hit the table.

The headline read, "Four found dead, appear linked, authorities baffled."

He continued to read. Apparently police had found four people dead the previous morning, each one of them was decapitated. The heads were unaccounted for. An autopsy had not yet been performed to test for the presence of drugs or other chemicals that could further link the deaths. Authorities were not ruling out a serial killer. Two of the victims were related and found in the same house. The other two victims were strangers with no apparent connections, found separately in neighboring areas.

The identities of the four had not yet been released, but rumors said that one of the men was local millionaire, Jonathan Koenig. Calls to his office for comment were not returned.

"Holy crap," said Luke. "Was that real?"

He sat bewildered for a few minutes, just staring at the article, reading it over again. Eventually his alarm rang, which meant it was time to leave for work. He headed out to this car, started it up, and put it in reverse. He looked in his rear view mirror to see if anything was behind him as he was backing up. There in the mirror was the hooded figure from his dream, just smiling at him.

www.ingramcontent.com/pod-product-compliance
Ingram Content Group UK Ltd.
Pitfield, Milton Keynes, MK11 3LW, UK
UKHW041918190726
13854UKWH00003B/1305